WARNING TO YOU, READER PERSON

Total Mayhem books
are **not** normal books.

They are full of:

weird stuff,
some **cuckoo** stuff,
lots of **new** stuff,
and some **funny** stuff.

Unexpect the expected.

ISBN 978-1-338-77044-5

1 2021

Printed in the U.S.A.   23
First printing 2021

Book design by Lisa Swerling & Ralph Lazar

TOTAL MAYHEM BOOK 3 WEDNESDAY – THE FOREST OF SECRETS

CONTENTS

Created by Ralph Lazar.
Fertilized, watered, and
pruned by Lisa Swerling.

THINGS YOU NEED TO DO
BEFORE YOU READ THIS BOOK

Read to the bottom of this list
first before doing any of these.

[1] Tap the top of your head twice.
[2] Blink 5 times.
[3] Wiggle your toes.
[4] Stand on one leg and baa like a
    sheep 5 times.
[5] Lie totally flat and moo loudly
    like a cow 5 times.
[6] Tap the top of your head again.
[7] Make yourself comfortable.
[8] Okay, now that you've read to the
    bottom of the list, ignore all
    except number 7.

USE THE ALMANAC

There's tons of new info in this book. If you see something **underlined in the story** and you don't know what it is, it'll be in the Almanac, which is at the back of the book.

Or online at
total-mayhem.com/almanac

FINAL INSTRUCTIONS

Read this book with:

[1] an open mind

[2] an open window

[3] an open box of TREATS.

CHARACTERS

Wednesday

The Forest of Secrets

Forest-Scallywags
Enemy fighters

Ms. Greenacre
Zip-Lining teacher, and her pet eel, Derek

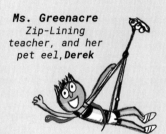

Dash Candoo
Hero of these stories

Mrs. Rosebank
Principal of Swedhump Elementary

Ms. Ozniak
History teacher

Umbahorra
Friendly but deadly (see Almanac)

Rob Newman
Dash's best friend

Gronville Honkersmith
Classmate

Greta Gretchen-Hoffer
Classmate

Shereena Aska-Lonka
Classmate

Collum Ollum
Classmate

Ms. Grimstead
Chief Library Officer

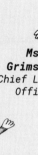

Mr. Steadyneck
Potted-Plant Balancing teacher

Mrs. Wobblethorpe
Bed-Jumping teacher

Devil-Cat
Enemy fighter

Mr. McYawn
Really Boring Class teacher

Jeanjean-Jeanjean-Jeanjean Johnson
Classmate, twin of Jonjon

Jonjon-Jonjon-Jonjon Johnson
Classmate, twin of Jeanjean

Chapter 1

Before
Breakfast

It REALLY annoys me when
one gets into a
Total Mayhem Situation
before breakfast.

Which is exactly what
happened to me this
morning.

I had just poured
myself a glass of
<u>osteop milk</u>...

and was sitting down
to a warm slice of
<u>pizzup</u>.

I was just thinking how
pizzup is my **absolutely
favorite food**...

...when my <u>KB-15</u>
started flashing **red.**

Danger was close!
I didn't even have
time to prepare.

I went straight to the
front door.

Opened it...

...nothing.

How strange.

KB-15s are normally 100% accurate.

In fact, all KB-15s come with a *Lifetime Warranty.* There are no documented examples of KB-15s failing in **any** situations **ever,** unless of course the batteries have not been charged. I make sure mine are **always** fully charged. You should too. And if you don't have a KB-15, you should get one. Really.

Then I heard a rustle in the <u>smellephant grass</u>.

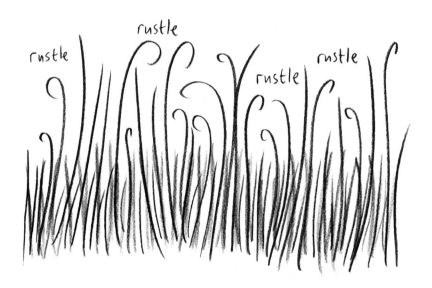

Smellephant grass grows wild where I live. And I guess you know why it's called that, right? Because <u>smellephants</u> **LOVE** it.

And there they were.
Suddenly.

Five
<u>Forest-Scallywags</u>!

This was not good.

Forest-Scallywags are
MASTERS of camouflage.

They immediately began to attack using
Move #18,854:
The Rolling Starfish.*

STEP 1: Launch   **STEP 2:** Inversion

STEP 3:
Starfish

*This is a HIGHLY dangerous and very technical move. **DO NOT** try this at home without consulting the <u>Almanac</u>.

There was only one
thing for it.

I counterattacked with
Move #10,266:
The Weird Face Move.

This involved pulling
extremely weird faces,

which made the <u>scallywags</u>
start to **laugh.**

The more they tried to stop
laughing, the more the
Rolling Starfish **wobbled,**

until...
TOTAL COLLAPSE!

They lay in a hopeless pile
for a few stunned seconds...

...and then staggered
off, defeated.

That was close, but at
least it was over.

Now I could get back
to my breakfast.

Or so I thought...

...because the next
thing, **out of the blue,**

an **umbahorra**
appeared!

And now comes the
totally TERRIFYING
bit...

...it *GRINNED.*

WHY is this so scary, you ask?
Well, **IF YOU HAVE TO ASK,** you
haven't read the Almanac.

If you **HAD,** you'd know...

...that umbahorras have
THE most **disgustingly awful**
smelly breath.

So bad that it can actually
knock you out.

I had to act and I had
to act **fast.**

I pulled out my <u>Transformer</u>...

pressed the button...

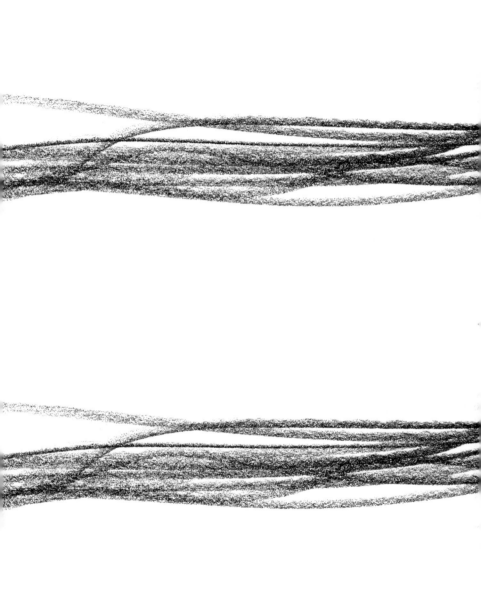

...and transformed the
umbahorra into a cupcake!

It went scurrying off after
the Forest-Scallywags.

I then went back inside and
finished my breakfast.

It annoys me having to eat
cold pizzup, but there really
wasn't time to heat it up.

I didn't want to be late
for school.

Chapter 2

Bed-Jumping

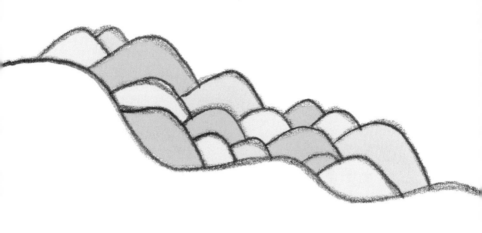

After breakfast
I headed off to
<u>Swedhump Elementary</u>,
**the Best School in
the World.**

I was totally excited
because our first class of
the day was going to be a
new subject with a new
teacher.

We'd been told the teacher
was a lady called
Mrs. Wobblethorpe, and she
would be our
BED-JUMPING instructor.

BED-JUMPING?
BED-JUMPING!

Let me explain. There was a
worrying incident on a
school trip recently.

Class 133F had gone on
Marine Biology Week.

This involves living for
a week on **Angel Island** and
studying fish and everything
to do with the ocean.

And on Angel Island,
they got to stay in a
6-star HOTEL.

But apparently, and I know this is going to give you a big fright, some kids did **NOT** spend every spare moment jumping on their hotel beds.

This picture is actual proof. Look at them just sitting there!

What??

How can you NOT jump on
your bed, especially in
a hotel situation?

When Mrs. Rosebank,
our **AMAZING** principal (who, in
case you don't know, is *totally*
and *completely* **INVISIBLE**),
found out about it, she was
worried that the reputation of
the school was at stake and
made the decision to hire a
Bed-Jumping teacher.

I've made a
decision!

*This is Mrs. Rosebank making
her decision.*

Enter
Mrs. Wobblethorpe.

Apparently, she used to own
**the World's Second-Most
Amazing Hotel,**

so it goes without
saying she's jumped on
quite a few beds.

And she was SO nice.

She was *very*
complimentary about
my jumping

and was also
impressed with Rob's
Double-Loops

and Greta's
**Grinning
<u>Triplosaults</u>.**

But mainly she was very
busy fiddling in the
vomit-colored briefcase
on her desk,

and taking
a lot
of phone calls.

It all seemed a *little weird*, but I guess it was because she was probably a little *nervous* and didn't know the school rule of

NO PHONES IN THE CLASSROOM.

NO PHONES IN THE CLASSROOM

All in all it was a
really fun class, but I
couldn't help wondering:

What was in the
vomit-colored briefcase?

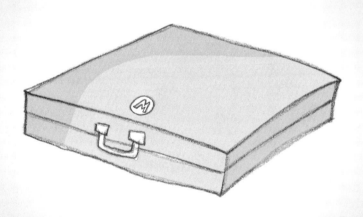

Chapter 3

Zip-Lining

The second class of the day was one of my all-time favorites:

Zip-Lining

with *Ms. Greenacre.*

She was the
World Zip-Lining Champion
in 2014, and is
VERY FAMOUS.

(You may think that's a scarf around her
neck, but it's not. It's actually Derek,
her pet eel. Ms. Greenacre never goes
anywhere without Derek.)   *47*

For five years after her World Championship win, she was so famous that she actually had to have bodyguards.

Even when she was riding her <u>noncycle</u>.

A noncycle is a nine-wheeled bicycle, in case you were wondering. Not to be confused with a <u>nonsencycle</u>.

Normally our lessons are
in the school's
<u>Zip-Lining Emporium</u>,
which is
fantastic.

But Ms. Greenacre explained that since they were doing some repairs there, we'd have the lesson in <u>Moremi Forest</u>, instead.

Moremi Forest is a **huge,** *beautiful,* and quite **mysterious** forest that borders our school.

Rob and I have spent a lot of time exploring it, and we know some *incredibly secret things* about it, which I'll tell you about another time.

← The forest is said to extend over 3,000 miles to the west.

Outer wall of our school

When we got to the entrance, we were surprised to find it blocked. A sign on it read:

NO ENTRY
FOREST TEMPORARILY CLOSED DUE TO
<u>INVIZIZZ MIGRATION</u>

<u>Invizizzes</u> are a kind of
stinging insect
and can actually be
quite dangerous.

If an invizizz stings you,
the part of you that got
stung goes invisible briefly,
for an hour or so.

53

If you get stung by
several, you might go
completely invisible
for a few hours.

In April last year,
Mr. Hogsbottom's cousin
got stung by a mini-swarm
of twenty-two invizzizes.

↗

This is him
an hour after
the attack.

↖ And this is
him three
hours after
the attack.

It is believed that if you get stung by a swarm of over a thousand, you could go **invisible** *forever.*

Some say that's what happened to the principal of our school, *Mrs. Rosebank*, leaving her **permanently invisible.**

This is a photo of Mrs. Rosebank on a recent fishing trip.

Anyway, I hadn't
realized it was
invizizz migration
season.

How *disappointing*.

We went <u>smushroom</u>
picking instead, which
was great, since
I love smushrooms.

Smushrooms are like
mushrooms but
DELICIOUS.

**They actually taste
like chocolate.**

While we were picking, I
heard some humming noises
from deep in the forest.

Invizizzes?

But invizizzes don't hum —
they buzz.

It almost sounded like...
MACHINES?!!

And then I thought about
it some more.

This was actually **NOT**
invizizz migration season
at all.

There was something VERY
fishy about that sign!

Chapter 4

RBC
(Really Boring Class)

Our third class of
the day was RBC
(Really Boring Class)
with Mr. McYawn.

He is the world's most
boring person, which is
why he is the perfect
teacher for RBC.

Today's lesson was
about...

...actually, it was so
boring I'm not going to
tell you what it was
about, as you'd fall
asleep for sure and miss
the rest of the story.

Rob and I agreed we needed to get back to Moremi Forest and see what was happening there.

So I took out my
Slow-Motion-ifyer
and set the classroom to
setting 8, which is
REALLY slow.

A Slow-Motion-ifyer allows you to slow down everything around you, *but not you yourself.*

So for example, if you're in a **pizzup-eating competition** and you need more time, you can just slow the whole room down and, voilà, take as long (and eat as much) as you want.

munch
munch

slow
motion

slow
motion

We'd bought ourselves
some time, so we got into
action.

We ran as fast as we could
to the <u>Hammaphore Tree</u>
outside Mrs. Rosebank's
office.

Normally I'd just tell you to
check the Almanac for more
about why Hammaphore Trees are
SO AMAZING, but to save you
flipping to the back, I'll
quickly tell you here.

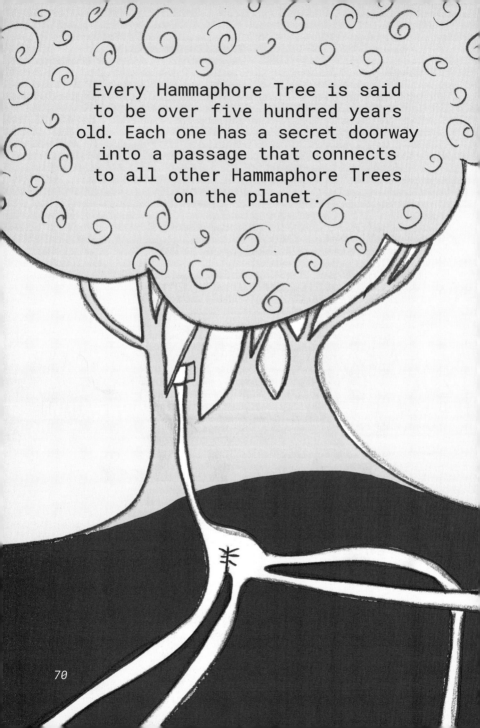

Every Hammaphore Tree is said to be over five hundred years old. Each one has a secret doorway into a passage that connects to all other Hammaphore Trees on the planet.

Several Hammaphore Trees grow
in Moremi Forest, in addition to
the giant one just outside
Mrs. Rosebank's office.

A secret way into the forest!

Rob and I are the only people
who know this, so we had to
make sure we weren't spotted by
Mrs. Rosebank.

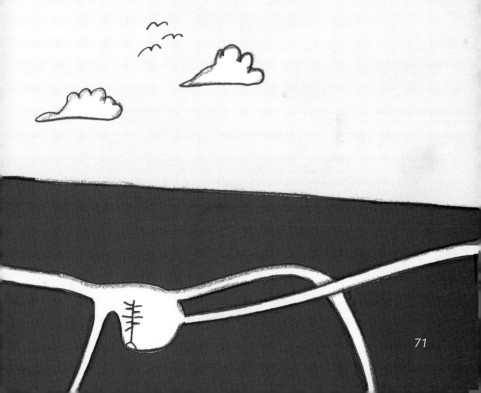

Because she's invisible, the only way we know whether Mrs. Rosebank is **in** her office or **not** is via her flag system.

If she is there, she raises a yellow flag. If she's not, she doesn't.

Which is obvious, because if she's not there, how can she raise it?

FLAGPOLE

PRINCIPAL ZOFIS

There was
no flag flying!

A.M.A.Z.I.N.G.!!

Up we climbed and
in we popped.

Once inside, it was well
signposted.

MRS.
ROSEBANK'S
OFFICE

MOREMI
FOREST
ENTRANCE

EIFFEL
TOWER

CENTRAL
PARK

We didn't have far to go.

In any case, distances inside the <u>Hammaphore System</u> are MUCH shorter than real-world distances.

This meant we could get to Moremi Forest in a flash!

We emerged right at
the entrance.

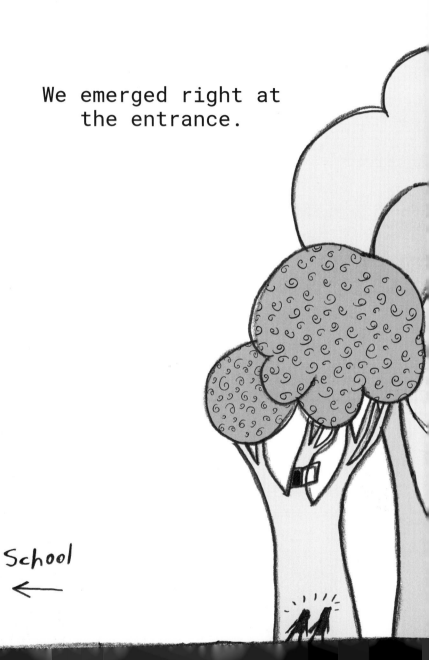

School
←

Everything looked messy. There were tire marks all over the place — trucks or machines or something had been here VERY recently. DEFINITELY something **very** fishy going on.

We followed the tracks into the forest. The weird humming noises were getting louder and louder, but there were no machines to be seen at all.

Suddenly, we heard a
mysterious rustling in
the trees...

...and we had an eerie
feeling that we were
being watched.

Back in class, nobody
had noticed we'd been gone
because of course they
had all fallen fast
asleep.

Mr. McYawn droned on and
on about something,
in slow motion.

It was quite a funny
sight!

Chapter 5

History

On the way to history,
we noticed a weird line of
leaves on the ground. With
a few minutes to go before
class started, we decided to
follow the trail.

The leaves led all the
way to...

...Mrs. Wobblethorpe's classroom!

We tried the door, but it was locked.

VERY SUSPICIOUS.

It was the perfect
chance to try out my new
<u>Zap-Flattener</u>!

In case you didn't know,
when someone is zapped by
a Zap-Flattener, they go
totally and completely
flat for sixty seconds.

This gave Rob enough time to slide through the gap under the door and into Wobblethorpe's classroom.

Just then Ms. Ozniak, our history teacher, walked past.

"You're going to be late for history, Dash Candoo!"

What should I do?

① Spill the beans to Ms. Ozniak and lose the chance to find out **what was behind that door**,

or

② Head to class and leave Rob to let himself out of the room when he'd finished?

I decided to follow
Ms. Ozniak back to
class. I knew Rob would
join me soon enough.

Ms. Ozniak is the world's
best history teacher.

Her lessons are so exciting
and real, it feels as if she
has traveled to each place
and time herself. In fact,
many people believe she is
actually a **time traveler.**

There are rumors that she had a cup of tea on top of the pyramid in Giza the day after it was finished,

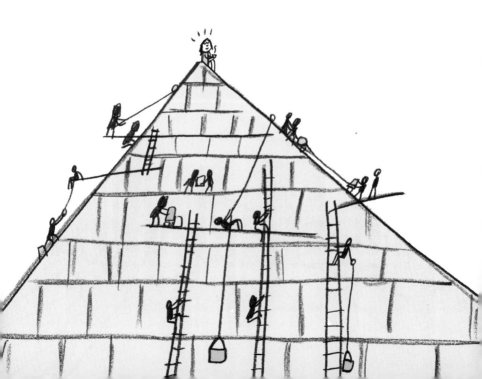

a cup of coffee on the *Titanic,*

ICEBERG

ICE CREAM

and a cup of <u>choc-hotlitt</u> (similar to hot chocolate but better) on the summit of Everest with Hillary and Tenzing in 1953.

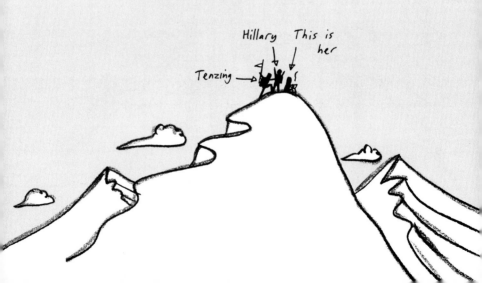

Hillary   This is her

Tenzing →

Today's lesson was "The History of Ants in Antarctica," which I was pretty excited about.

Meanwhile, Rob was relieved to find Wobblethorpe's classroom empty.

The trail of leaves led to her desk, on which sat the vomit-colored briefcase.

Rob opened the
briefcase.

There were all kinds of
plans for what appeared to
be a large building.

And maps of a forest.

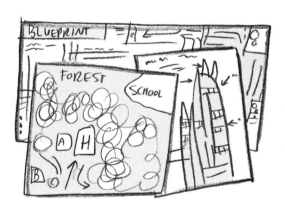

Rob quickly activated his
Cranio-cam, took photos, and
tele-transferred them
straight to my Cranio-cam.

But then, there
was the sound of a key
in the door,

and
Wobblethorpe
herself appeared.

"WHAT ARE YOU DOING HERE?" she quelled (question-yelled) as five Forest-Scallywags leapt out from behind her in a flurry of leaves.

Rob was caught.

Wobblethorpe sprayed him
with <u>goop-goop</u>.

Very not
good-good!

The evil woman then grabbed
her briefcase and marched
out with the Forest-
Scallywags close behind.

It all happened so quickly
that Rob didn't have time to
ping me an emergency signal.

And now he was trapped,
deep in goop-goop!
Absolutely **NO SIGNALS** could
get through that!

The history class turned
out to be **very** short
because there are no ants
in Antarctica, despite the
continent's name.

But more importantly —
where was Rob?

He should have been back
ages ago!

I was hoping he'd be
waiting for me outside
history, but he wasn't.

So I ran as quickly as I
could to Wobblethorpe's
room. The door was still
locked. I called for Rob.

Nothing.

I opened up my TTD (<u>Transponder Tracking Device</u>) to see if I could pick up a signal from him. Rob and I carry concealed TTDs at all times. This lets us locate each other in emergencies. ***And this was one.***

I pinged him.

Nothing.

Hm, how very strange.

**AND
WORRYING.**

Where the heggleswick
was Rob?!!

Chapter 6

Library

Our next class was Library
with Ms. Grimstead.

I ran to the library
building, hoping Rob would
be there to meet me.

Ms. Grimstead used to be the Chief Library Officer of the **UNRLEAM** *(the United Nations Royal Library of Everything & More).*

For that job she had to memorize the exact locations of *32,000,000,007* books. Impressive.

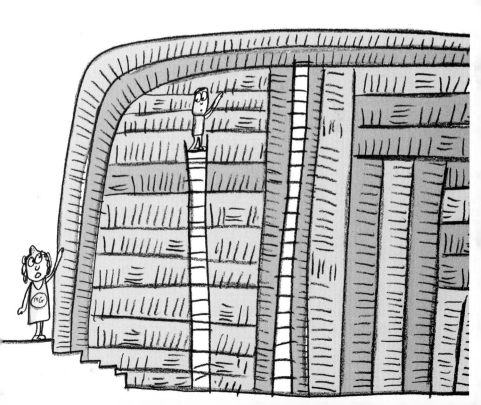

Now she's
Chief Library Officer
of Swedhump Elementary.
A high-status position
if ever there was one.

Oh.
Did I mention the
head lump?

As well as being the world's most famous librarian, Ms. Grimstead can be **COMPLETELY AND UTTERLY TERRIFYING,** depending on whether her head lump is throbbing or not.

Because, yes, she has a big
green lump on her head.
Some people even speculate
that there might be
another Ms. Grimstead
growing out of the lump.

And if there is, does THAT
Ms. Grimstead have another
Ms. Grimstead growing out
of *her* lump?

When it throbs, she's
REALLY grumpy.

When it doesn't throb,
she's just slightly
grumpy.

Luckily, today Ms. Grimstead's head lump was not throbbing. In fact, it was barely even green.

Ms. Grimstead was very happy about this. She told us that she was going to take a **celebratory nap**, so we could have a free class.

Which was just as well, as Rob had still not turned up.

I had to find him.

I downloaded the photos
Rob had tele-transferred
to my Cranio-cam.

The first looked like a
plan for a building.

I zoomed in...

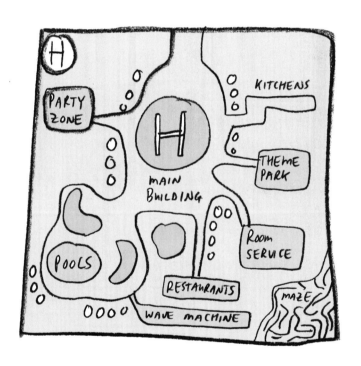

it was plans for a
hotel.

A BIG HOTEL.

The other photo was a map of
a forest — Moremi Forest!

But lots of the trees had
been crossed out and a big

H

was written in the middle.

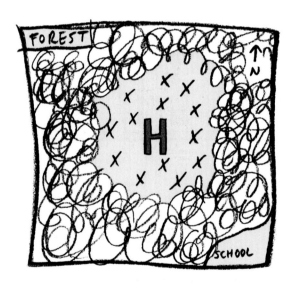

I suddenly realized:
They were going to get rid of
the forest and build a hotel
in its place!

If they'd captured Rob,
that's where he might be.

I had to get over there.

No time to lose!

I <u>warp-vortexed</u> myself in
a trillisecond to the *H*
on the map.

Oh no! So many trees had
already been cut down!

I stepped into the clearing
and looked around.
Still no sign of Rob.

No sign of
anything.

But then...

...my head hit something hard.

Something very hard.
Like a wall.

But there was
nothing there!

WHAT?!!

I suddenly got it!
SOMETHING INVISIBLE!

They must have already
started building the
hotel and thrown an
<u>invisibility shield</u>
over everything: the
hotel itself and all the
machines and diggers
and cutters.

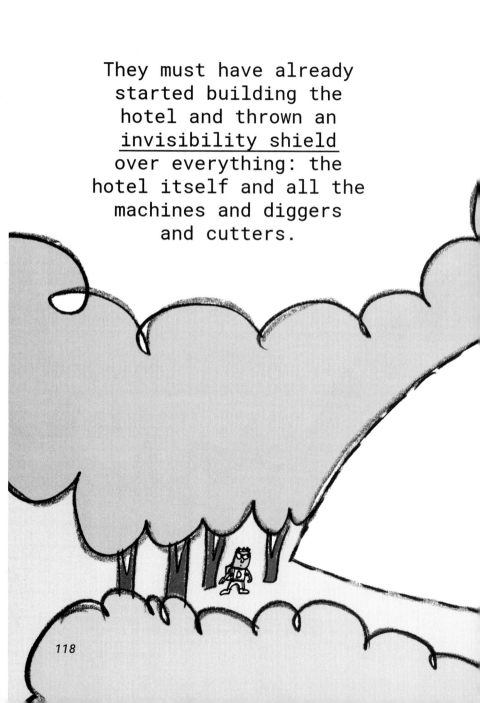

They were building it
secretly so no one
would stop them. The
fake invizizz migration
sign had been there to
keep everyone out!

I couldn't spend too much
time thinking about that —
I had to **find Rob!**

I looked behind bushes,

under bushes,

behind rocks,

behind bushes behind rocks,

under bushes behind other
bushes,

and behind bushes behind
rocks that were behind
bushes (near other bushes).

I also
looked
behind
trees,

behind rocks
behind trees,

behind bushes
behind trees,

behind bushes
behind other
bushes behind
rocks behind
trees,

up trees,

behind rocks
up trees,

behind
bushes up
trees,

and
behind
trees on
top of
trees.

No sign of Rob anywhere!

And then I had that
feeling again.
Of being watched.
I looked around.

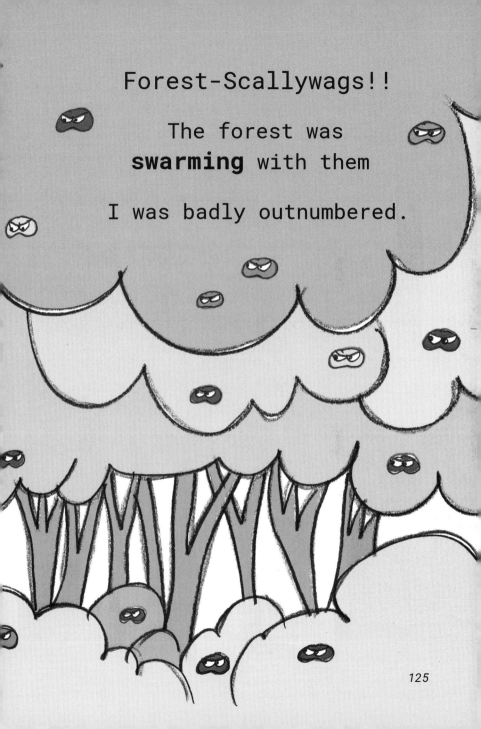

So I warp-vortexed out
of there as fast as
I could!

Back to Swedhump
Elementary and the
last class of the day.

Chapter 7

Potted-Plant Balancing

Luckily, I arrived just as
the class was starting:
Potted-Plant Balancing
with **Mr. Steadyneck.**

He won the
<u>World Potted-Plant
Balancing Championship</u>
in 1958.
He's VERY old.
And VERY nice.

Today's lesson was
cactus balancing.

Collum Ollum is the most talented potted-plant balancer in the school and knows almost every <u>potted-plant balancing move</u> in the Almanac.

He went straight in for a decuple (that's ten pots!).

Mr. Steadyneck was very impressed.

Greta Gretchen
Hoffer tried an
octuple (8).

Success!

Jonjon-Jonjon-Jonjon Johnson
tried the same and it failed.
Jeanjean-Jeanjean-Jeanjean
laughed at him so Jonjon-
Jonjon-Jonjon threw a pot at
her. Luckily, it missed so there
were no tears.

Then Shereena
Aska-Lonka
balanced
a momentous
novemdecuple
(19)!

Collum (he's quite
competitive) decided to try
a quadragintuple (40)...

...and succeeded!

SPECTACULAR!

Meanwhile, Gronville Honkersmith was messing around as usual, and put an empty pot upside down on his head and then couldn't get it off.

It was totally and completely **stuck.**

Mr. Steadyneck told us
to do our own thing
(class canceled!) as
he rushed Gronville off
to the medical room.

What a day this was
turning out to be.
If only I had Rob to
discuss it with...

...I had to find him!

His last known
whereabouts were inside
Mrs. Wobblethorpe's
classroom. I had not
checked INSIDE the room.

So that was my next
destination.

I ran back to the classroom
and tried the door.

STILL LOCKED.

Now I moved fast.
I pulled out the
Zap-Flattener, pointed
it at myself, and...

ZAP!

I was as thin as a piece
of cardboard! A pretty
weird feeling,
I must say!

I slipped under the door.

As soon as I arrived, I
realized that something
had gone wrong,
very, very wrong...

Rob was totally
TRAPPED in a ball of
goop-goop!

But I was SO relieved
to see him that I
actually burst out
laughing.

He did look
VERY funny.

I used my <u>MRX-34 Laser</u>
to cut him free.

"Very unlike you, Rob!"
I smiled.

Rob was annoyed but
also relieved!

He told me all about
Wobblethorpe and I shared
what I'd found out from
the maps.

We agreed we had to get
back to Moremi Forest and
stop Wobblethorpe and the
Forest-Scallywags
ASATP
(As Soon As Totally
Possible).

Luckily,[*] I had an Almanac
in my backpack.

We looked up the best
way to deal with
Forest-Scallywags.

*Actually, it wasn't luck. I **always**
have an Almanac in my backpack. You
should do the same. Because you **never**
know when you might need it. You just
never know.

I could tell you
right now
what we found,

or you could look up
Forest-Scallywags in the
Almanac and try to work it out
yourself,

OR YOU COULD JUST KEEP READING!

Devil-Cat
Huge double-tailed black cat
that always lands up on the
wrong side of the law.
Tends to partner with criminals.
Fears nothing but fruit.
However, he loves vegetables,
especially carrots.

Devil Nose Island
Devil Nose Island is the most secure prison ever
The entire perimeter is ringed by 27 krypto-we
fences, 11 of which are electrified. The wat
around it is freezing and full of shnarks
(which are more vicious than sharks);
flesh-eating, saw-toothed doublodios;
and killer electric rays. No prisoner
has ever escaped from it.

Dublifier
This copies (or doub
So for example, if
pizzup but you we

Forest-Scallywags
How common: Moderat
Special powers: C
Weakness: Laugh
nothing e
l grou
lo

We rushed over to the
library to find
Ms. Grimstead,
to convince her
to join us in our
**mission to save
the forest!**

Chapter 8

The Fight

In the library,
Ms. Grimstead was still
taking her **celebratory nap.**
The head lump seemed to be
throbbing ever so slightly.

What should we do?

If we woke her, it was
totally **certain** her lump
would begin throbbing
IMMEDIATELY and A LOT...

...and she'd never agree
to help.

Then I had an idea!
I pulled out my
<u>Dublifier</u>.

A Dublifier is a device
that makes an almost
exact copy of someone.

The double lasts forty-five
minutes, then disappears.

149

I zapped Ms. Grimstead,
and — YES! — *another* Ms.
Grimstead (MG2) appeared.

This one
was awake.

**And in a
good mood!**

We warp-vortexed to
the forest.

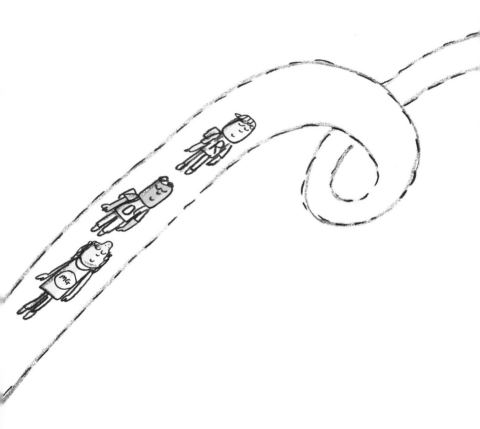

As soon as we arrived,
the Forest-Scallywags
began to emerge.

And then...

(you'll be able
to guess...)

Mrs. Wobblethorpe
herself appeared.

No surprise there.

And THEN guess who
appeared beside HER!

DEVIL-CAT!

Okay, that *was* a surprise.

"I am building the world's biggest hotel right here, and nobody will stop me," declared Wobblethorpe.

Devil-Cat grinned.

*"Especially two **silly little boys** and their **granny**,"* said Devil-Cat.

(OMG, he can talk. I'll never get used to that.)

"We're not silly little boys!" shouted Rob.

"And I'm NOT their **granny**," yelled MG2.

Out of the corner of my eye, I noticed something *very interesting*. MG2's lump had begun to throb.

Clearly, that *granny* comment had made her **very** angry.

Then she snarled.
Her lump snarled too.
The scallywags took a step
back, **trembling with fear.**

You will **now know** what
we found out in the Almanac!
Forest-Scallywags are scared of
only one thing:

ANGRY LIBRARIANS!

"There's just one of her,"
shouted Wobblethorpe,
"and so many of us.
GET HER!"

The Forest-Scallywags
advanced.

Then I had another idea.
A *brilliant* idea.
I took out my Dublifier,
pointed it at MG2, and
zapped her!!

MG3
appeared!!

Then I zapped both of them, and MG4 and MG5 appeared. I zapped again and again, until there was a whole herd of Ms. Grimsteads.

And their head lumps
were *really THROBBING.*

The Ms. Grimsteads
snarled.

The lumps snarled.

The Forest-Scallywags
ran away, *terrified!*

But that still left
Mrs. Wobblethorpe
and Devil-Cat.

We heard a loud
zipping sound and
Ms. Greenacre (and Derek!)
appeared out of **nowhere**.

They were a totally
terrifying sight!

Devil-Cat ran with a
yelp into the forest.

Wobblethorpe
(also yelping)
was not quite as fast.

Greenacre released
Derek.

169

Bang, on target!
Wobblethorpe was DOWN!

Derek wound himself
around her feet like a
rope, and she was
trapped.

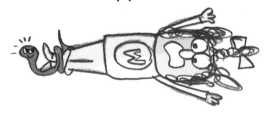

A **MAGNIFICENT** victory!
But there was still
work to be done.

Rob pulled out his <u>SPIN radio</u>
and called for assistance with
the wriggling Wobblethorpe.

I took out my
<u>Micro-Modulated Shrinkulator</u>.

Then we put on our
<u>Anti-Invisibility Goggles</u>.

Now we saw it.
The **INVISIBLE HOTEL**.
And it was already *HUGE*.

I turned the
Micro-Modulated Shrinkulator
to **full blast.**

From there, everything
happened really fast.

The hotel began to shrink.

Before too long
it was the size
of an actual pea.

A police <u>triplocopter</u>
arrived and carted
Mrs. Wobblethorpe off to
<u>Devil Nose Island</u>.

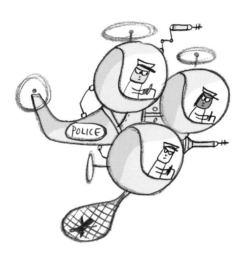

Ms. Greenacre, Derek, and
the Ms. Grimsteads cheered.
(And, yes, their lumps
cheered too.)

Ms. Greenacre and Derek waved
goodbye as they zipped off
into the foliage, and the
Ms. Grimsteads — all fifty-seven of
them — disappeared with a pop!

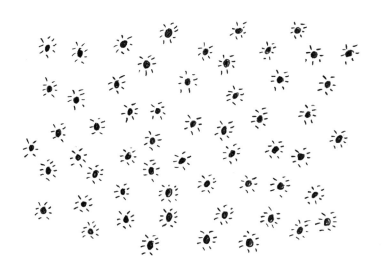

There are exactly fifty-seven pops here.
Count them if you don't believe me!

Rob and I warp-vortexed
happily back to school.

179

We arrived to find that Gronville STILL had the pot on his head and was surrounded by teachers trying to help him.

He was making very weird and loud rhinoceros noises!

Dr. Williams

Mrs. Zhonst

Mr. Steadyneck

Mrs. Belch-Hick

Mr. Darling (he left his pinkfish behind in his classroom)

Mr. Grodzinsky

Those noises were not quite
loud enough to wake
Ms. Grimstead, now the one
and only **_TRUE ORIGINAL._**
She was still fast asleep –
an epic celebratory nap if
ever there was one – and
making charming rhinoceros
noises of her own.

And then the bell rang.

What a day!

Time to go home!

ALMANAC

Almanac

The COMPLETE ALMANAC is the place where you can find out everything about Dash and his world. It's online here: total-mayhem.com/almanac. What you're reading now is the Book 3 Almanac, providing detailed information for Total Mayhem Book 3 only.

Angel Island

A small and very beautiful island smack in the middle of the

Atticus Ocean. There's only one structure on it: a hotel.
Fringed by a coral reef and warm water. With probably the world's most beautiful sunrises and sunsets.

Anti-Invisibility Goggles

Anti-Invisibility Goggles (AIGs) are an extremely useful tool. Dash and Rob usually carry them in their backpacks. They are

most effective for recently invisibilized things. So for example, if a Wrestle-Scallywag went into invisibility mode a few minutes before, the AIGs would pick them up. But if they went into invisibility mode a few weeks before, the AIGs probably would not. So the AIGs don't work on Mrs. Rosebank, who's been invisible for years.

Choc-Hotlitt

Like hot chocolate but better.

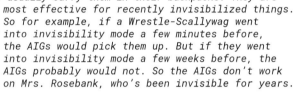

Hot Chocolate	Choc-Hotlitt
Taste: 8.3/10	Taste: 10/10
Flavor: 9.1/10	Flavor: 10/10
Smell: 7.5/10	Smell: 10/10
Overall: 8.3/10	Overall: 10/10

Cranio-Cam

Tiny, mind-activated camera embedded on the top of the head. Dash and Rob each have one. These cameras are so small that when unactivated they are almost invisible. To activate a Cranio-cam, all you need to do is think about it, and out it pops. Same goes for retraction.

They're waterproof, and their batteries last forever. Can only be embedded by registered members of the CCEI (Cranio-cam Embedding Institute). Photos and videos taken with them can be tele-transferred to other people who have Cranio-cams.

 ① ② ③ ④

Devil-Cat

Huge double-tailed black cat that always lands on the wrong side of the law. Tends to partner with criminals. Fears nothing but fruit. Terrified of watermelons. However, he loves vegetables, especially carrots.

Devil Nose Island

Devil Nose Island is the most secure prison ever. The entire perimeter is ringed by 27 krypto-web fences, 11 of which are electrified. The water around it is freezing and full of shnarks (which are more vicious than sharks); flesh-eating, saw-toothed doublodiles; and killer electric rays. No prisoner has ever escaped from it.

Dublifier

This copies (or doubles) something if you zap it. So for example, if you have just one slice of pizzup but you want two, just zap it.

Forest-Scallywags

How common: Moderate
Special powers: Climbing, camou-flage, wilderness survival
Weakness: Laugh very easily
Fear: Nothing but angry librarians
Typical group size: 5 or more
Operate alone? Yes
Maximum jump distance: 32 feet
Cleverness: 6/10
Speed: 7/10
Agility: 8/10

Goop-Goop

Nasty spray glue. Doesn't dry completely. Great for capturing people – just spray them and then they are stuck in the blob.

Hammaphore System

The Hammaphore System is the secret underground network that connects all Hammaphore Trees on the planet.
Distances inside the system are much shorter than distances in the outside world. This means travel inside it is really quick and efficient.

Tunnels and intersections are very well signposted, so it's almost impossible for a Hammafore System traveler to get lost. When new Hammaphore Trees grow, the signposts automatically update. Lighting in the tunnels is provided by natural soil phosphorescence, so no flashlights are needed.

Hammaphore Tree

Several Hammaphore Trees grow in the forest next to Swedhump Elementary. Each one is said to be over 500 years old. Every Hammaphore Tree has a secret doorway into a passage that connects to all other Hammaphore Trees on the planet. Dash and Rob are the only people who know this. Or so they believe.

SECRET DOORWAY

Invisibility Shield

Makes everything inside it go invisible.

Invizizz

Invizizzes are beelike insects that sting. They are completely silent and their venom causes localized invisibility. They only sting when they are grumpy, but unfortunately they are grumpy 77 percent of the time. The other 23 percent of the time they are asleep.

Invizizz Migration

Biannual event where tens of millions of invizizzes head south for the annual Invizizz Symposium and then north again to get home. No one knows what actually happens at the symposium.

KB-15

Imminent Danger Warning Device (IDWD)

KB-15 Flash Codes:
* Red — on-off 1-second intervals continuous: Imminent Danger
* Red — on 2s, off 2s: Imminent lightning storm
* Green — on 3s, off 1s: Pizzup delivery almost here
* Blue — on 5s, off 5s: Battery needs charging

Marine Biology Week
Each grade at Swedhump Elementary goes on a one-week marine trip every year. Involves travel by boat, submarine, and a stay at the legendary Angel Island Hotel. Everyone looks forward to it.

Micro-Modulated Shrinkulator
Highly sophisticated device that shrinks things. Only to be used if you have a Clearance Certificate, which requires three months of training. Once you shrink something with it, it cannot be undone. REPEAT, it CANNOT be undone.

Moremi Forest
A huge forest bordering Swedhump Elementary. Said to extend over 3,000 miles to the west. Several Hammaphore Trees have been found in it.

Move #10,266: The Weird Face Move
Deployed if you want to make your enemies laugh.

Move #18,854: The Rolling Starfish
Used exclusively by Forest-Scallywags. They form a circle by locking arms, then go vertical and start to roll. Very dangerous to encounter. Can be knocked over by spraying with water or making them laugh.

MRX-34 Laser

Small, concealable, very powerful laser.
Ideal for cutting through things.
Can also be used for communication.

Noncycle

Nine-wheeled bicycle. Ms. Greenacre has one,
purchased from Darwin Cycles. Runs so smoothly
that it is believed it was actually built
and tested by Humperdermus Ibis himself.

Nonsencycle

A nonsencycle is a ridiculous noncycle,
i.e., a nine-wheeled bicycle that doesn't
make a whole lot of sense. Collum Ollum
doesn't have one. He has two.

Osteop Milk

It's pretty easy to milk osteops. Their milk
tastes better if milked with one's left hand.
Doctors recommend one glass daily, to be
drunk between 7 a.m. and 8 a.m. If you drink
it after 8 a.m., you might get an upset elbow.

Pizzup

Pizzup is like pizza but different. And better.

Not only because it tastes better, but because one of the key
ingredients is hover-yeast, which allows the pizzup to levitate
(or float). So it can hover above a surface.

For example, if your desk is covered in stuff, you can have
a pizzup without any problems because it will hover above the
clutter. Or, if you're riding your quadcycle, you can get a
pizzup to fly alongside you for easy eating. They have been
known to hover at speeds in excess of 41 miles per hour.

Disappointingly, eating a pizzup doesn't have any effect on
your own gravitational pull. Collum Ollum once tested this by
eating a dozen pizzups. Big ones. It didn't make him float
but did make him vomit. Don't try it yourself.

189

Potted-Plant Balancing Moves

1: monuple
2: couple
3: triple
4: quadruple
5: quintuple
6: sextuple
7: septuple
8: octuple
9: nonuple
10: decuple
11: undecuple
12: duodecuple
13: tredecuple
14: quattuordecuple
15: quindecuple
16: sexdecuple
17: septendecuple
18: octodecuple
19: novemdecuple
20: vigintuple

21: unvigintuple
22: duovigintuple
23: trevigintuple
24: quattuorvigintuple
25: quinvigintuple
26: sexvigintuple
27: septenvigintuple
28: octovigintuple
29: novemvigintuple
30: trigintuple
31: untrigintuple
40: quadragintuple
41: unquadragintuple
50: quinquagintuple
60: sexagintuple
70: septuagintuple
80: octogintuple
90: nongentuple
100: centuple
1,000: milluple

Scallywags

There are many different types of scallywag. Each type has its own fighting techniques, strengths, and weaknesses.

Slow-Motion-ifyer

A Slow-Motion-ifyer allows you to slow down everything around you, but not you yourself. So for example, if you are taking an exam and you need more time, you can just slow the whole room down, and voilà, take as long as you want.

Smellephant Grass

Smellephant grass is a fast-growing, tall, greeny-yellow grass that can be found on open plains, in the tundra, and in savannas. Also in suburbs. And on mountains, in valleys, near lakes and oceans. So pretty much everywhere.

Smellephants love it because they can hide in it, and it gives great shade, tickles their backs, tastes delicious, and smells pretty good too.

190

Smellephants

Smellephants are a bit like elephants, but they smell better.
And I don't mean they actually smell better, I mean they
smell better, if you know what I mean. You don't know what
I mean?

So what I mean is they are better
at smelling than elephants because
they can have up to seven trunks.
Their favorite place to hang out in
is smellephant grass. Obviously.

Smushrooms

Smushrooms are like mushrooms. But better.
They taste like chocolate.
Grow on the eastern fringes of Moremi
Forest.

SPIN Radio

A SPIN radio (Secure Police Interface Neo-
mogrifier) lets the user communicate directly
with International Police Headquarters. Very few
exist and only highly trained experts are allowed
to use them. It folds up to the size of a small
pea. Rob Newman usually has one with him.

Swedhump Elementary

Dash's school.
Principal: Mrs. Rosebank
Probably the best school in the world.
Definitely has the best teachers in the world.
Named after the hump of a swed, a two-faced humped creature.

Tele-Transfer

Tele-transfer is the mind-activated transmission of digital
files between Cranio-cams. So for example, if Rob takes a photo
with his Cranio-cam and then wants to send the images to Dash
(who also has an embedded Cranio-cam), all Rob needs to do is
think about it, and the images automatically transfer to Dash's
Cranio-cam. He can then download them and see them as if they
are on the table right in front of him.

Transformer
A Transformer is a HIGHLY technical device. There are over 100 different types, and new models come out each year. Dash currently uses a Chobey-2020.

If you have FULL security clearance (level 15c), we will be able to tell you more. Dash's Transformer uses an RM66 high-voltage battery, which needs to be charged once a week. No more, no less. If charged more often than that, the Transformer becomes too powerful. So, for example, if overcharged when trying to transform a cereal bowl into a watermelon, it could actually transform it into a hippopotamus, which would be funny but probably not good. If charged less often than weekly, the Transformer becomes too weak. So, for example, if you wanted to transform a bicycle into a car, it might transform it into a wheelbarrow instead.

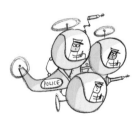

Transponder Tracking Device (TTD)
Dash and Rob always carry micro-versions of these. They allow them to find each other in emergencies — provided the device has been activated.
So, for example, if Rob gets captured but is unable to activate his TDD, he won't emit a signal.

Triplocopter
Triple-helicopters invented by G. & J. Tarrow Siblings Inc. in 2010. The equivalent of three helicopters stuck together. They are sixty-one times faster and seventeen times more powerful than regular helicopters, though more complicated to fly. The test pilot of the first version was James Hogsbottom, who teaches paper airplane class at Swedhump Elementary. There have been no reported triplocopter crashes to date.

Triplosaults
Triplosaults are triple somersaults.

A Grinning Triplosault is a triple somersault while grinning.
A Grinning Jellybeanified Triplosault is a triple
somersault while grinning while eating a jelly bean.

The categorization goes as follows:

Somersault (single somersault)
Doublosault (double somersault)
Triplosault (triple somersault)
Quadrosault (4 somersaults)
Quintosault (5 somersaults)
Hexasault (6 somersaults)
Septasault (7 somersaults)
Octosault (8 somersaults)
Nonosault (9 somersaults)
Decosault (10 somersaults)
Nonononosault (99 somersaults)
Nonononononosault (999 somersaults)
Weirdosault (failed somersault)
Gronvosault (somersaulting into a wall – Gronville
    Honkersmith has been known to do this)
Plumbersault (when Mr. Plumtree does a somersault)
Summersault (a somersault in the summer)
Wintersault (a somersault in the winter)

Umbahorra
Large, friendly-looking creatures with a lovely smile but a
devastating grin. This is due to their halitosis (stinky breath).
Their breath smells so bad it can actually kill you.

Warp-Vortex
A Warp-Vortex allows the warpee (owner)
plus sub-warpee (passenger) to move from
one place to another in a trillisecond.
Warp-Vortexes are typically backpack-
mounted. Pocket versions do exist but
are quite expensive.

Each Warp-Vortex has its own password,
which the users will not share under
any circumstances (so don't even ask).

World Potted-Plant Balancing Championships
Highly competitive annual event.

List of select champions:

1958: Mr. Steadyneck
2000: Constance Noring
2001: Oliver Sutton
2002: Eileen Dover
2003: Ben Dover
2004: Jim Nazium
2005: Barb Dwyer
2006: Mike Raffone
2007: Sheila Tack
2008: Mona Lott
2009: Anita Bath
2010: Olive Yew
2011: Hosyuh Snumplewidge
2012: Humperdinck Pinsnoffian
2013: Augustus Pinsnoffian
2014: Horatio Pinsnoffian
2015: Anna Larm
2016: Mika McLara
2017: Joshua & Theodore G.W. Smith
2018: Siena Rennie
2019: Gabriel Klein
2020: Eli Mockton

Zap-Flattener
Flattens things temporarily.
When a person is zapped by
a Zap-Flattener, they go
totally and completely flat
for sixty seconds.

Zip-Lining Emporium
Huge zip-lining park at Swedhump Elementary.
Actually the world's largest.
Designed by Ms. Greenacre.
Has over 2,700 different zip lines.

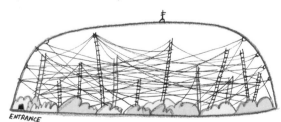

ENTRANCE

194

MAZES

Help Dash get to Rob
via Carrot 27b.

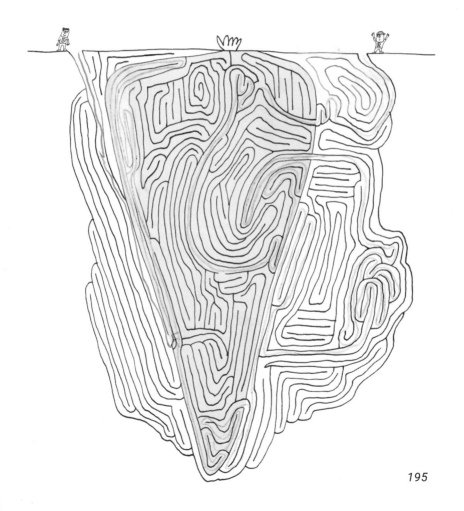

This invizziz hasn't stung anyone in a week, which means she's about to get shouted at by the **IIC** *(Invizziz Inspection Committee).*

Then she spots Mrs. Wobblethorpe's left elbow. Can you help her reach it?

Devil-Cat is *terrified of* **fruit**.

Help him get from **HNC1**
(Hairy Nostril Cave #1) to
HNC2 *(Hairy Nostril Cave #2)*
without encountering any
WATERMELONS (his worst!!).

Mr. Darling has been fussing over his pinkfish so much that they got **annoyed** and are *hiding* from him.

Could you reach them if he paid you **$12.37**?

ABOUT THE CREATORS

Ralph Lazar and Lisa Swerling live in California.

Ralph made up the Dash stories (inspired by wrestling his godson — Dash!) and did the drawings. Lisa shaped the stories into this book.

Ralph and Lisa are New York Times *bestselling authors, and the creators of the popular illustrated project* Happiness Is . . ., *which has been translated into over twenty languages and has over three million followers online.*

Their studio website is lastlemon.com

Ralph is also a painter and Lisa makes miniature worlds in boxes.

Ralph's art website: ralphlazar.com

Lisa's art website: glasscathedrals.com

FOR DASH CANDOO, EVERY DAY IS . . .
TOTAL MAYHEM!